TOTAL FLUFF

TOTAL FLUFF

By:
Nancy Przybylowicz

ARPress
ILLUMINATING IDEAS
EMPOWERING VOICES

ARPress
45 Dan Road Suite 5
Canton MA 02021

Hotline: 1(888) 821-0229
Fax: 1(508) 545-7580

Ordering Information:
Quantity sales. Special discounts are available on quantity purchases by corporations, associations, and others. For details, contact the publisher at the address above.

Printed in the United States of America.
ISBN-13:   Paperback   979-8-89330-969-0
                eBook   979-8-89330-970-6

Library of Congress Control Number: 2024902534

Table of Contents

DUMPSTER DIVE

My brother and I were hungry. So hungry, in fact, we didn't remember when our last meal was. One time when we were out riding our bicycles we smelled food by the local diner, because that's where they put the scraps. We were headed there now.

First, we had to make sure there was no one around. When the coast cleared, we ran to the back of the trash bin. My brother crouched down, and I used his back to hoist myself up and over the ledge. Then he handed or kinda threw the flashlight in – it was dark in here. Right away, I noticed it had a funny odor not familiar to me.

First, I'd look through the dry stuff, but it was kinda semi-moist all over. I found a Styrofoam container! As I opened it, only a few French fries, I threw it down.

"Hurry Bobby! I think I see a police car!" my brother screeched.

"Shh!" I scolded, "Not so loud they'll hear us!"

I quickly shoved away piles of garbage searching for food.

Jackpot! I found some old, wrapped, steak sandwiches. I threw them out to my brother. I stopped, panting, to catch my breath. In. Out. In. out, I breathed. Wait a minute, it sounded like I had a cough or a hoarse throat.

I held my breath. It was still going on. I wasn't alone. I got real scared.

"Billy, there's someone in here. Maybe it's a rat"

"Bobby, maybe someone threw somebody in there."

"Quick get me out! Now!"

"No. Go see who or what it is."

"Get the police. I'm afraid." I said.

Never mind. I went over to the whimpering sound and started to dig. Finally, after loads of dirty trash I was able to reveal black fur.

It was a small dog, half alive. I lifted her out on my tippy toes and my brother reached her out from the other side. Then I gingerly grabbed the top, metal edge and swung my right leg up so my foot curved and caught the edge, then I reached my right arm over the top, swung myself out landing on my backside. "Let's eat!" I thought.

Billy was offering the dog some of his newly acquired sandwich. The dog just licked and looked a little scared.

"He's gonna pass out if we don't get him to the animal shelter."

I chewed some food and spit it into my hand, then put it into the dog's mouth. He swallowed.

The animal hospital was way across town. We would need Dad to drive us. Or, maybe we could convince him to let us nurse her back to health. I had pillaged a baby bottle, leash, and an old tennis ball out of the trash. We piled our food and dog into our bicycle basket after we had put some crinkled newspapers down in the bottom to cushion the dog's lame body from jarrings of our bicycle ride. We had a pet!

THE REVEAL

It had been true that the two boys and their sister, Sarah, had wanted a pet cat or dog around the holiday season the year before. In fact, they had begged their dad for one when they found out most of their classmates either had a pet already, or were getting a brand new, cute puppy or kitten.

Now was their chance to convince their parents to allow them to keep this newfound friend.

"Hi, mom!" greeted the boys as they pulled up their bike in the driveway. Out of breath from pedaling so fast they panted, "Guess what!"

"What's new?" said Mom.

"Mom, you'll never believe what we found in the trash!" Bobby said.

"Why? What were you doing snooping in the trash?"

"We were hungry and looking for something to eat."

"I just went grocery shopping," said Mom, "I finally got paid. What did you find?"

"A dog," Billy said.

"Absolutely not. You can't keep him." said Mom,

"You'll see."

"Can we at least ask Dad?"

"Yes, but a dog is a lot of work. It's expensive to get shots and go to the veterinarian. Plus your Dad is out of work and my job barely pays the bills."

Discouraged, the boys planned to ask their father when he got home from job hunting. Meanwhile, they got help from Mom.

"First, let's see this pup," asked Mom. She walked over to the bicycle basket, carefully with gloves on she lifted the lid, "Phew, this isn't a dog, it's almost a corpse!"

She picked the dog up under its front paws and held it up like a rabbit. It opened its eyes. They were smooth and stony black. It managed a feeble bark.

"We'll give it a bath first."

"Can we help?"

"Sure."

"Then we'll try to feed it and when your father comes home we'll take it to the animal doctor."

We all got chairs, Sarah too, and stood around the sink basin. Mom used some tearless shampoo and lukewarm water and we scrubbed, making a zillion bubble. Then we rinsed with the sink hose. We got a clean towel for the dry off. We rubbed and rubbed, then got a brush and hairdryer. It smelled good.

But here's a surprise for you, he turned out to look two sizes bigger and all fluffy with clean hair and his new color was, well, white!

Then mom gave him some milk and meat. He ate some and then fell asleep.

Now, to wait for Dad to come home.

"Don't forget, your sandwiches are on the table." said Mom.

EXPLAINING TO DAD

After the dog took a nap, the kids couldn't resist touching the dog. They petted it, brushed it, and hugged it. Bobby said it looked hungry.

"Mom, can we feed it?"

"I have one of your old baby bottles," said Mom.

She filled it with cream and the dog made like a baby cow. It sucked and slurped until there was no more. In fact, Mom filled it three times and not a drop left. Then the dog fell into a deep sleep. The oldest brother, Bobby, said, "Who knows how long the dog was in the dumpster before we rescued him. It must have been more than a day, because he was so skinny and hungry."

Billy and Sarah agreed and wondered who could be so cruel to a helpless animal. They watched, protective over the dog as he slept. Their reverie was interrupted with a "Ding, ding." It was the doorbell, Dad was home now. They ran to get his hugs and kisses at the door.

"Guess what. Guess what," they pleaded.

"What?

"We found a dog."

"A dog!" Dad drawled excited. "How'd you get a dog?" The dog barked. Little did the kids need to know that Mom had called him to warn him.

Bobby and Billy both started to talk at once.

Dad said, "Let Bobby talk first." Billy looked at Bobby, even though he was the little brother, he felt that since he found the dog he should talk first.

Bobby was afraid to tell Dad the story since they weren't allowed by the diner or the dumpster.

"No, go ahead Billy," said Bobby.

"All right," said Dad, "talk Billy."

There was a long period of silence, then Billy spoke.

"I jumped into a trash can and there was a noise. I thought it was a person but someone threw out a good dog. Now we have him. Can we keep him, please Dad? We found him all by ourselves."

"All right, but only if you boys and Sarah do all the upkeep. And I promise you, he will be high maintenance. By the way, why did you jump into a trash can?"

"We were hungry," said Bobby.

"You know you are not allowed. You smell like the Parkway diner."

The boys were afraid they'd be punished, but Dad said, "Since you rescued a dog, you did a good deed. You're off. Go have fun and try to let the dog play."

"Can we keep him?"

"As long as you promise to look after him. You'll need to feed him, bathe him, walk him, and pick up after him when he goes to the bathroom. Between the three of you, it should be a piece of cake."

"Yay," the kids responded.

"But first, we'll have to take him to the veterinarian to make sure everything's okay."

After dinner, they piled into the car and went to the animal hospital. Dr. Greese was really good with pets.

"We found a dog," Dad explained.

"Okay, no worries. First we'll see if she's already owned." She found no missing reports for a dog of its description, and she chip checked.

"I'll let you know if anyone files a new missing report. My guess is that someone stole the pet as a prank and threw it in the trash. Not uncommon when pets become sick and a problem."

"Next we'll give it its rabies shots and all other necessary vaccines. I'll give it a deworming pill, and you can have a complimentary flea collar. Oh, and it's a she."

The dog was examined and given a clean bill of health.

"It would be a good idea to put an address tag on it. I'll make one for you."

"What's its name?" All the kids wanted to give it a name but Dad let Sarah.

"Since she's so fluffy, I'll name her, Fluff." They were thinking more on the lines of Bailey, or Maxine, but they told her, "That's a great name, how'd you think of that?"

"After the bath, she fluffened up," Sarah said.

A new identification collar was put on and they went home. They couldn't wait to tell all their friends at school that they were the proud owner of a new pet dog. The children doubted Dad's decision so they asked again.

"Can we keep him?"

"I don't know. What are the reasons that you want a pet dog?"

Bobby said, "All the kids at school have dogs. That's all they ever talk about."

"I want a dog because he's cute and cuddly," Sarah said.

"We will hug her and give good love to her," said Billy.

"He'll bark at the mailman, too." He knew Dad didn't like the mailman much because he was always confusing the neighbor's mail with his.

"What else?" asked Dad.

They all chimed in, "He'll bark at prowlers. He'll fetch your slippers and Sunday newspaper! Please can we keep him?"

Dad had heard somewhere that keeping a dog was good for the self-esteem of youngsters. "Okay," he finally answered after much thought. "As long as you keep up your end of the bargain and take care of him like you promised."

THE UNKEEPABLE DOG CHANGE OF FORTUNE

For the rest of the summer, into the fall and winter, the kids grew accustomed to their new pet. They played, cuddled, taught, and trained. They scooped, fed, scrubbed, and walked. They talked, laughed, shared, and showed, with their friends. But then Dad shared a bombshell.

"Kids, I've lost my job. The company downsized and I'm no longer needed by them. This means a tightening of our budget, and frankly, Fluff is expensive to feed and support on a shrunken budget. Therefore, our cable, phones, and dog have to go. Until I find a new job."

"Eow," Sarah started to cry, pout, and stomp her foot.

"No," she wailed with her face scrunched up trying not to cry.

"Dad, no," Bobby and Billy said in unison.

"You kids think about it and come up with a plan of attack. Then I'll let you know if I think it's doable."

"What are we gonna do," the kids said to themselves.

"Well, if it's about money, maybe we could start our own business or something. To help raise funds," Sarah said.

"I like the idea, but you need money to make money," said Billy.

"I know," said Bobby. "We can do odd jobs such as babysit, mow lawns and water plants, house sit, take care of other people's pets while their away."

The next day was Saturday. They told Dad and Mom while sitting at the breakfast table of their plans.

"Oh, what a wonderful idea," Mom said. That settled the matter, they were in business. Mom too, decided to clean houses, cook, and babysit while Dad was doing his job search because with a five-person family budget, funds can only go so far.

One day when Dad had struck-out many times, Fluff brought him the newspaper. He found a job from an ad in the classifieds.

The kids had been taking care of Fluff for a long time now. Almost a year. They were doing well but were getting tired. The dog needed to be walked early in the morning around six am to avoid making a mess. When they overslept, they would have to do a lot of cleaning. They walked the dog and let her run in the yard. The droppings were needing to be cleaned up good or they would get on their shoes with a knowing squish feeling on their foot. Then the smell would show up. Then they would have to get a stick or toothpick to clean their sneaker treads. Plus, they got into trouble when a bare spot showed up on a neighbor's lawn. So, they had to be extra cautious when the dog had to go and carry around extra grocery bags for clean-up.

Now, on top of all this, they had to do neighbor's chores to help support their pet. It was going to be a lot of hard work. But the love of their pet seemed to outweigh the uphill struggle they faced.

They also wanted to socialize their dog with other dogs. So they rounded up pets and owners that wanted to come to their dog's birthday party. They really didn't know when their pet was born so they picked July fifth, easy to remember since it was the day after Independence Day. They ran it by Mom, and she said yes.

So it was still summer and Sarah, Bobby, and Billy had to find some easy income. Mom mentioned to Sarah about Mrs. McBeeble having a vacation coming and no one to take care of her pet bird.

"Why don't you go across the street and introduce yourself? Tell her I sent you and she'll give you an interview," Mom said.

I don't want to go, Sarah thought to herself. I don't know her. I feel shy. What if the bird flies the coop on me? I'll never get over it. She told her brothers of her plight.

"But you can go," they said. "We have an old fishing net, if it gets out, we'll catch it and put it back."

She really loved Fluff so she went by forcing herself over her fears. She waited what seemed like hours staring at the door. Seconds, minutes ticked by before she felt stronger and ready. Then she pressed her finger onto the doorbell. Several chimes sounded in a melodic tune. Nothing. One more time and if nothing she would leave. But just as she was turning to go, the door creaked open and a feeble, gentle, gray-haired, stooped woman opened the door and said, "Yes?" in a warbly, effortful fashion.

"I'm inquiring about the pet job," said Sarah.

"Oh you are Susan's daughter," she said. Susan was the first name of her mom.

"Yes."

"She told me about you. Come in. Thanks for waiting. It takes me long to get to the door these days."

Bobby, Billy, and Sarah went to school the next day, they couldn't wait to tell their friends that they too now had a family pet.

"Guess what Traymore," at recess they said.

"What?"

"We got a new dog!" They said in unison.

"What kind?"

"A white fluffy dog we named Fluff."

"But what breed?"

"What's a breed?"

"A species of dog."

"We can go to the library today to find out," the teacher was listening to their conversation.

"We'll do this as our science period lesson.

Later that afternoon they went to the library. They sat in a circle by the rocking chair.

"Boys and girls," she began, "Who has a pet dog?" A handful of children raised their hands.

"Who can tell me the breed or name of the dog's species?"

Almost all of the hands went down. Of the remainder there was only two children who had their hands up.

"Okay, Traymore, what is the breed of your dog?"

"German Sheppard."

"Good. A breed can be determined by a dog's family history. Certain traits over the century, such as hunting, protecting, beauty, and good nature, were genetically engineered to produce certain types of dogs over the years that could be helpful to humans. Bobby, Billy, and Sarah have a new dog they rescued and are not sure of the breed. We are going to help them find out. We have to find a book that shows pictures of breeds, then we can determine their scientific name of their dog. We'll look under the card file for the grouping books on dogs."

They managed to find ''All About Dogs," by Carl Burger. The teacher read to them from the book and showed pictures. Then a picture of their dog came up.

"That's her, that's Fluff!" It was a West Highland white terrier. Its main job was to scout foxes and protect animals and plants on farms.

The children said, "When we found it, we thought it was a black-haired dog because it was so dirty from being on the street. We washed her and she turned white."

The teacher said, "Keep us updated on your dog. We'd love to hear about how you take care of her and how you train her. Class dismissed."

The children ran home. They pedaled as fast as they could to go home. Out of breath they panted, almost like a dog.

"Mom, mom! We know the breed of our dog."

"Well, take a deep breath and let me know."

Trying to catch her breath, Sarah said, "It's a, breath, West, breath, Highland."

Bobby breath, "White."

Billy breath, "Terrier."

"I'm glad you found out what it is. Just make sure you train her well and care for her good."

"As soon as you finish your home lessons you can walk the dog around the block, feed and water the dog, brush her, and give her some ball chase exercise. Don't forget a scooper and bag."

That day, they finished their homework in record fastness.

Sarah cleaned the bowls and gave it water and chow.

"I better not give her too much food," she thought. She learned what amount was good. The dog was hungry, she started munching as soon as the sounds of the pieces hitting the bowl occurred. "Wait, Fluff." The dog stopped and she added a little more.

The boys went to get the leash, scooper, bag, and ball. They waited while the dog ate. When she was finished they put the tether on her collar. "Let's go Fluff."

Bobby, being older would hold the leash until they got accustomed, or used to, walking Fluff.

Billy and Sarah would do the pickup duty, you know what I mean.

It was a bright and sunny day. There were few clouds in the sky. The dog would pull this way and that, a natural explorer. They kept it to the sidewalk.

"Hello Susan," they saw their neighbor in her flower garden.

"Oh, I see you've got a new friend."

"Yes, her name is Fluff and she's a West Highland white terrier."

"Ruff," said Fluff. One day Fluff hid a bone in her garden.

"Well, you kids better be off and give your pup some exercise."

Sarah, Billy, Bob, and Fluff set off down the road. Billy said as he reached for the leash, "My turn."

Bobby yielded the leash. Billy had a grin on his face as he held the tether with Fluff on the other end. "This is fun," he thought. The dog stopped here and there, and Billy was having the time.

Then Bobby wanted the leash back.

"No! I want to hold the leash."

"What about Sarah?" She hasn't been given a turn.

So Billy gave the leash back to Sarah. A few minutes later Bobby swiped the leash from Sarah. She instantly started crying.

"Oh, stop that Sarah. We've wanted this dog for a long time and you're getting tired. What if it runs away? You'll have plenty more times to hold the leash and walk her."

"Okay," she broke out between sobs. They gave the dog a short rest and then they gleefully trod on. They stopped by the park and saw some ducks. They saw other owners with dogs on leashes. Fluff was sort of quiet all the time. She sniffed and followed scent leads. Then they saw Fluff start panting and whining and sat down. They pulled at the leash, but Fluff was like a stone and wouldn't budge.

They tugged and tugged and commanded, "Walk, Fluff, walk. Let's go home." But Fluff sat motionless.

"How are we going to go home without Fluff?"

"I know," said Bobby. They had walked too far and Fluff was sick. Bobby reached down and scooped up Fluff in his arms. He gently and gracefully carried Fluff home.

As soon as they got there they gave her fresh water. Then she went to her dog bed and laid down.

They told mom what had happened. "Just make sure you bring some water next time and don't go too far," she responded.

They told her all about Susan, the neighbor, and how there were other dogs who liked Fluff at the park. They also told her about the fighting over the leash.

"You all can't hold the leash at once. Divide the block up between here to Susan's house, then there to the park, and then the park home. That's about in thirds. Decide that Sarah will go first, then when she gets tired, Billy and then Bobby will make sure to bring her home or carry her if Fluff is tired."

"Makes sense," they all said in unison and went to help Dad set up dinner because it was Mom's night off. But they still fought.

The next day was Saturday, and the weekend began.

Sarah got up extra early to feed Fluff the dog chow. She started to pour into the dog bowl when Billy grabbed the box out of her hand. "You did it yesterday, my turn!" Sarah began to cry.

Bobby showed up next and grabbed the edge of the box with Billy. Sarah's eyes moved back and forth to Billy and Bobby as she watched the tug 'o' war battle. Just when Billy was pulling hard, Bobby, on purpose, let go sending kibble high into the air and all over the kitchen Mom had just cleaned.

"Bobby, look what you just did!" Billy screamed. Mom and Dad were not far behind.

"You kids will have to learn to take turns. Feeding also involves cleaning the food bowls and sweeping the area."

"Yuk," said Sarah.

"Yes, and also, the yard has to be picked up, it's a mess."

So then Dad designated Bobby do the walks for a week, Billy do the feeding, and Sarah pick up the yard. They would rotate jobs the next week. Billy would walk, Sarah feed, and Bobby pick up and then switch again after that week was over.

Sarah had an idea. Mom's perfume smelled good and Fluff's business didn't.

"I know," said Sarah.

"I'll sneak her perfume and fumigate the yard."

Sarah looked for a good time Mom would be out of her room. Mom started gardening. She tiptoed up the steps. When she was about to go into her Mom's room she heard footsteps. It was Bobby. He would tell. "What are you doing?"

"I'm looking for something for Fluff," she half lied.

"Hurry up, we're going to have a play session with her."

When he turned his back, she ran into the room and snatched the decorative glass bottle named Patra. The yellow level in it was only a tiny bit down. It must be new. She dropped it into her jacket pocket and ran. Sarah sprayed the whole yard as she cleaned it. "That takes care of that awful smell," she thought.

Sarah went to Billy with her problem, "I used Mom's perfume for the dog."

"I have an idea," said Billy. "We'll fill it with water and lemonade, she'll never know. Guaranteed."

"Okay." She ran and got the mini funnel. Billy procured the water and lemonade. They filled the bottle and it looked just like the real thing. They put it back right where it was before.

Days went by and they knew Mom had used the perfume because the level went down. She still didn't know. Billy and Sarah looked at each other and shared a secret laugh.

Fluff then was given a bath. They used special tearless shampoo and just a little bit. It sudzed up good. Then they used a warm hair dryer and then they brushed a little. Fluff gained a little weight and was more filled out and healthier. She ran free in their fenced in yard. The kids tried to train Fluff by repetition, and it worked!

They taught her sit, paw, fetch, and come. When they said sit, they gently pressed on her bottom and she sat, they did it a lot and she eventually learned. They rewarded her with a dog cookie. They did the same with paw, or shake, fetch, and come. They were so ecstatic that the dog could be trained and knew commands. They were proud that they had trained the dog with little help but Mom's food reward suggestion. They were a hit with their school friends when they found out. Maybe they would go to a dog show.

A week went by and Mom and Dad were going on a hot date. Mom had used the perfume.

"Dad, how do you like the perfume you bought me for my birthday?"

Dad sniffed near Mom, "O, lovely. You smell great." Sarah and Billy stifled a giggle. It must have been a combination of hard soap and hair spray that fooled Dad because he and their Mom were clueless. They had gotten away with their plan, for now.

Sarah, Bobby, and Billy ate, slept, lived, and breathed Fluff. They really loved this little dog. They took good care of her most of the time, but it began to be hard for them to remember their jobs and they didn't do them perfectly. That's where Mom stepped in and helped them. She sometimes walked the dog in the morning and fed Fluff. She helped pick up-u the yard when needed.

Fluff had this wild affection for Mom and Dad. Whenever they came home from a car trip, Fluff jumped and wagged her tail at them. She ran and barked at their car. It's as if she knew they were her main caretaker.

One day while the children were all in the house with Fluff after school, Fluff was resting nibbling at a chewy toy. Bobby was playing a nasty video game and Billy wanted to play doubles, but Bobby wanted to see how high he could get points. A fight ensued.

"Bobby could you please let me try?" Billy said.

"No, leave me alone. I've never got this good before."

So, Billy reached for the control. Fluff growled. Then Bobby almost did something to Billy, but Fluff moved into action and bit the controller out of Bobby's hand and ran off with it, wire trailing behind.

Fluff told himself now was his chance. Those other owner's never thought he could do something right, so they threw her into a trash bin. But he had watched the young-uns and knew when a fight could break out. Therefore, he removed the item that caused the situation. He ran under the bushes where he had dug a secret, all-purpose hole, he dropped the game control in and quickly covered it with dirt and grass for camouflage. Perfect, thought Fluff. Now to run to the other end of the yard because now they would come looking for her. She pretended to dig so they would think she buried the thing there.

Surely enough they came a runnin'. They got a shovel and dug like mad gravediggers but there was nothing in there.

"Now see what you've done," said Bobby impatiently wanting to finish to see his high score, not being pleased with his younger brother Billy.

"I'm sorry," said Billy starting to sob.

"I think Fluff was hungry," said Bobby, "Maybe we'll be going to the vet after dinner.

When Bobby, Billy, and Sarah's Mom and Dad came home from work Billy ran to tell them what had just transpired. "Mom, Dad, Bobby wouldn't let me use the video game and," but Bobby cut in.

"Billy ruined the video game."

"I paid a lot of money for that contraption," said Dad.

"You're always fighting and we don't like it. From now on, you'll have to earn your own money to buy a new video game if you stop fighting. Also, I've lost my job today and you'll have to earn your own funds for taking care of Fluff, because I can't afford it. If not, she had to go."

So, Mom met with Sarah, Bobby, and Billy.

"We don't need a video game," they chimed, "We'd rather keep Fluff."

"Okay, but you'll have to find a way to earn a little money for her food and toys."

"I know," said Sarah, "We can walk the neighbors' dogs and help them with their garden weeding. Get their groceries when they can't." They asked Ms. Susan to help them because she seemed to know a lot of the neighbors and she didn't.

They went over to Susan's house. "Ms. Susan will you help us, Dad's lost his job and we want to keep Fluff. But we need our own money."

"So how can I help you?"

"We need to know what odd tasks we can do to earn tips so that we can pay for dog food."

"Oh, Ms. Doe needs her parrot looked after because she's going on a two-week vacation."

"Thanks Susan."

So they waddled on over to Ms. Doe's house and rang the doorbell.

A frail old lady with a gray bun slowly opened the door. She recognized the children. "Come on in, I've got milk and cookies waiting." The children went in but left Fluff tied to the porch post because they weren't sure if the bird would mind.

"Sit down and have a cookie," Mrs. Doe said.

When they were all seated, Ms. Doe asked, "What can I help you with?"

"We need to help you take care of your pet when you go on vacation."

"Oh, thanks for offering. How do you know I was going?"

"Ms. Susan."

Ms. Doe remembered back and knew she had told Ms. Doe. "Okay." She told them the dates and time she would be away and then explained how to take care of Chappy.

"Every day, you must first clean the cage with dish soap, water and a sponge I will leave out for you. I would prefer if Sarah would do this. Then you must put paper into the bottom of the cage to line it. Then you must put in seeds three fourths full into the feed cup and H2O into the water dish. Put a few drops of this yellow liquid into the water. That's because we've taken the bird out of its natural environment and makes up for what it lacks.

"Thank you," loudly chirped Chappy. "Thank you," the bird kept repeating it a weird, combined language sort of way.

She quickly explained where to find the house key and ushered Sarah out of the house along with the two boys.

"Thank you. I'll send you a post card."

Sarah, Billy, and Bobby left, they were now in business.

Billy thought up an idea. He knew all the other dog owners in the neighborhood plus he knew the mail carrier. What if he could deliver the mail plus walk their dogs at the same time! He asked the mail carrier. "Only people registered to carry the mail are allowed. Tampering with mail delivery is a federal offense."

"Oh. I didn't know."

"That's okay," the mail carrier said, "You can deliver the circulars of advertisements for ten cents a copy, but you'll have to follow me."

"Great!"

The postman called the postmaster to make sure it was allowable, and it was.

"Mom, I'm going to deliver the mail, and get paid. Plus, I'm going to walk dogs at the same time."

Mom wasn't too sure it would be doable, but she agreed.

"Just be careful."

Bobby thought of an idea, most of the neighbors were elderly in his neighborhood. What if he would be able to do things for them that they needed, like buy groceries or cook, clean, or other things they couldn't achieve themselves? They could tip him for these odd jobs.

So, even though it wasn't Halloween, he knocked on some doors and explained his situation. "My Dad lost his job and we just recently got a new pet dog. We have to pay for her ourselves. But we don't have any money of our own."

"Sure, sure, you can mow our lawn once every two weeks and I'll give you forty dollars," Mrs. Susan replied.

So, he got one lawn mowing job. Bobby didn't like mowing lawns. He asked some others and got to be an aide to them and buy groceries, make beds, and clean houses. Since it was summer, he could do something different each day of the week. Groceries Monday with mom and distribute what people needed. Lawn care Tuesday, house cleaning Wednesday. Cooking Thursday. It seemed overwhelming that he could do all this for a young boy. But he would undertake these tasks and do the best he could.

Dad was so proud when he came home from work. "I'm so happy you all found employment. Be professional and do the best you can. Mom and I will help you succeed if you have problems or run into issues." And so, summer began.

It was her first day on the job taking care of Chappy and Sarah was excited. She had always fantasized about a bird using her finger as a perch and being at one with nature.

She found the hidden key and opened the front door. Mrs. Doe had left the large cage covered. She put on gloves and uncovered Chappy. He squawked, "Up and running, up and running." Mrs. Doe had informed Sarah that the late Mr. Doe had been into teaching Chappy how to speak and that Chappy would occasionally emit phrases that sounded incoherent.

As she reached into the cage the bird pecked at her finger. "Ah." Sarah exclaimed. No one had told her the bird pecked! She was afraid to do her job. No one told her, her fingers looked like food. If she only had her mother's suede gardening gloves. Someone had told her that if she felt afraid the animal would sense it. So, she kept calm and joined the bird in conversation, "Nice day out isn't it," this distracted the bird and she was able to remove the dirty paper. The bird lifted its head and eyed her as it incorporated the new message. "Do you miss momma?" She changed the seeds and began cleaning out the cup. "Are you thirsty?" She cleaned the water cup and put it back. Chappy took a little sip as he dipped his beak in the cup. "See you tomorrow."

"Goodbye." Chirped Chappy.

She couldn't wait to tell her family how brave she was. She had reached into the cage and almost got pecked but then she engaged Chappy in a conversation and he no longer tried to do it. He probably didn't recognize her smell because Chappy had low eyesight. She had never been this close to a bird before. Maybe if Chappy liked her he one day would perch on her hand.

When the family gathered at the table at dinnertime, Father asked how her day went.

"Sarah how'd it go with Mrs. Doe's bird?"

"Everything went fine except the bird tried to peck my fingers and I didn't have protective gloves."

"What did you do?"

"I tried to have a soothing conversation with Chappy. He can talk."

Billy and Bobby tried hard to stifle giggles but couldn't.

"That's very clever and brave of you Sarah, quite an accomplishment."

"Thanks Dad," said Sarah.

Billy's newspaper route started tomorrow. He had everything he needed, backpack for the papers, leashes and dog treats, etc. He got Fluff's leash on and got the three other neighbor's dogs ready, two were medium size, and one was large. The postman came by and put his circulars in his backpack. He was going to follow the mailman. It started off okay. The dogs didn't strain at the leashes, and they were moving fast and at a good pace. But the mailman had to wait when the dogs sniffed around.

"I'm going to have to move on without you because I'm losing time waiting for you."

"Okay." Said Bill a little scared. He only had twenty-five houses and would earn two dollars and fifty cents. He carried on, but the dogs were hot and thirsty. They were panting and didn't like going back and forth to where the mailboxes were kept.

Finally, the inevitable happened, he accidently let go of the leashes as he was reaching in his backpack. The dogs darted away.

"Wait!" screeched Billy. He dropped his backpack and scrambled after the dogs.

"Come back here."

The more he chased, the more they ran, jerking the ends of their leashes just out of grasp, taunting him playfully. Finally, he called them holding out his hand with the treats. They saw the treats but it failed to bribe a return. Suddenly they were gone out of sight. What was he going to do? He started a search. He looked at the park, the corner store, the post office. Nothing. He knew one place he hadn't looked. Where would I go if I were a dog and hot and thirsty? Sure enough, when he got to the neighborhood swimming pool, there they were splashing and frolicking around. They probably had gotten in through a hole in the fence, since the pools were not open for the season yet.

Billy quickly returned to home base and told his mom.

"Mom, the dogs ran away."

"I'll call the neighbors."

Billy started to cry. What about Fluff. She too had run.

It turned out that all the three dogs had made it back to their owners through their homing skills.

Knock knock at the front door. It was the mailman.

"I thought you might like more than the mail delivered." He reached in his mail bag and pulled out a white dog. It was Fluff. Then he handed Billy two dollars and fifty cents for handing out advertisements. The neighbors would wait to the end of the week and pay him later because he had let their dogs run away. Next time he wouldn't do two things at once. He would walk the dogs first, and then deliver the circulars. That would make it much easier. His dog day was done, or had it just begun?

Bobby volunteered to take care of Ronny, and elderly sick person in the neighborhood who couldn't get around much. She would pay him twenty dollars a day for helping her. It was ten am. Ronny came downstairs after dressing and saw Bobby. "What's for breakfast?" she asked.

"Anything you'd like," replied Bobby.

"How about two scrambled eggs, toast, and coffee."

Bobby was unsure of his cooking skills but remembered back to how his mom made them. There was one part he needed help on.

"Do you beat the eggs first or after they're in the pan?"

"I like them runny, so in the pan."

Bobby began, he cracked the eggs into a cup, removed the shell, turned on the stove and Ronny told him where the pan was.

"They turned out pretty good," said Ronny after she had finished breakfast.

"Now if you would make my bed and start the wash. Oh, and finish the breakfast dishes."

Bobby did just as Ronny asked. He cleaned the breakfast dishes, made the bed and started doing the wash. It took him nearly all morning. Then he sat by Ronny and took a break.

"How's your dog Fluff doing? You must really care for her to take on a job during summer when kids usually like to be free."

"Yes, we've always wanted a pet, especially a dog. Now that we've grown attached to her, we'd hate to lose her."

"Dog is man's best friend and having her will teach you all responsibility."

Bobby agreed, "Yes it does."

"Will you make me a sandwich?"

It was lunchtime already and he had talked all morning with Ronny about his family and his friends in the neighborhood and at school.

He fixed her a sandwich, chips, and drink which she ate readily. Then she gave him a list of things she needed at the grocery store and a twenty-dollar bill. He rode his bicycle over to the corner store. Mr. Sanly was working on putting the food cans away.

"How can I help you?" Bobby showed him the medium size list and they gathered the items needed. But Bobby came up ten cents short. "That's okay Bobby. Pay me next time." Bobby put the grocery bags in his bike basket and delivered the items to Ronny.

She helped him put the items away and then paid him for the day's help. "See you tomorrow."

Bobby stopped by the grocery store on the way home and gave Mr. Sanly the ten cents.

"Thank you Bobby, you're conscientious. Take care."

Bobby's first day on the job was a success.

When the children all returned home from their respective jobs, they put all the money in a sauce jar Mom had cleaned out for them. They could dip into the jar whenever they needed to buy supplies for Fluff, such as food or flea spray.

Billy walked the four dogs which included Fluff. Sometimes they dug up grass on Mr. Rasseter's lawn. Mr. Rassetter was a retired postal worker. He came out when the dogs were in the process of messing with his lawn. "Stop this right away. What is the meaning of all this."

"I'm sorry sir. The dogs for some reason seem to like to destroy your lawn."

"Don't let them near my house or lawn again, understand?"

"Understood."

One day, Billy was out walking the dogs again. He got distracted by some people on bicycles and the dogs were off and running. He quickly went to the community pool, but someone had patched up the spots where the old holes were so if the dogs tried to get in there they wouldn't be able to. So, he began looking in the neighbors' back yards who had pools.

"No! Not Mr. Rasseter's pool." Bobby ran as fast as he could run to the man's house. "No, Mr. Rasseter, don't hurt the dogs."

"If you don't get them out of here, I'll hurt you."

Billy quickly rounded up the dogs. Mr. Rasseter agreed to let Billy wash his car free of charge for the rest of the summer as need be in payment for the use of his pool for the dogs.

PART TWO

Then Dad came home from his job search. "Any luck honey?" Mom hopefully asked.

"Not today," he sadly intoned.

But Mom flew into a rage. "Why don't you try the places I told you to? Our bills are piling up. What are we going to do?"

"We'll ask my parents to help out until I find something."

"Oh. Bright idea. How will we pay them back?"

"I don't know. We'll invite them over for dinner more. I'm middle-aged no one wants to hire a fifty-five-year-old male."

"With your experience, sure they do. Go get a hair dye and cut. Get new fashionable eyeglasses. And go to the thrift store for a new suit and tie. I'll get my sister to tweak your resume."

It seemed to cheer Dad up that they were all on his team. But what they all didn't know was that it was the beginning of the Great Recession and jobs like his were scarce. He did everything they said to no avail.

"What are we gonna do?" Sarah asked her brothers.

"I have an idea," said Billy, "We can go to the library and look in the old newspapers or microfiche and see if anyone lost a dog during that time. They may have advertised a reward such as ten thousand dollars and we could give back Fluff and get the money. Then we all wouldn't have to work so hard taking care of the dog, plus help Mom and Dad out until they find money or a job."

"I like that idea," complimented Bobby to his younger brother. Billy felt so pleased he finally got a kudo.

"We'll be rich," said Sarah.

So, the next day they planned to make a special trip to the library to see what happened in town the day that Fluff was found. Hopefully, some news or clue would help them find some answers. Nobody would just dump a cute and good little dog like Fluff in the trash for no good reason.

The next day the three children snuck away to go to the town library. They remembered the date they had found Fluff. It was May 23rd. They got the microfiche bin for the local newspaper. They had trouble setting up the magnifying lens.

"Martha, can you help us?" they asked.

"Surely." The librarian helped the set up the microfiche reader. "There you go." They scanned the old newspaper. There were the usual articles of the day concerning the school district and township projects. But there was no article in the classifieds of a lost pet. There was an interesting article about a small traveling circus that was in town but that was all. They were stumped.

"That's it!" said Billy. "It must have been related to the circus. I'm not sure how. But don't they train animals in the circus?"

"Yes," said Bobby. The next time the circus was in town it would be at the end of the summer. They would go and inquire about the dog then. In the meantime, they worked at their summer jobs and help their Mom do her household tasks such as cooking and cleaning. They took care of Chappy, Ms. Ronny, and walked the neighborhood dogs. Then they played with Fluff in the sprinkler and gave her a bath. They fed her, walked her, and picked up after their dog. When they were bored, they took her to the park to play with the other dogs in the dog park.

They sort of got tired from time to time and would leave Fluff alone in the fenced in back yard. She would retreat to her doghouse and rest.

When it was time to take care of Fluff, they had trained her to do tricks.

Sarah commanded sit. The dog whined. She gently pressed on the lower back of the dog. "Sit," called Sarah. The dog stood still, then panted and sat, "Sit, good dog." The dog stood again, "Sit." But she still did not know what to do. She pressed hard on Fluff's back and it sat.

"Don't do that too hard," said Billy.

"Sit, good dog," said Sarah. The dog stood up and whined, she was getting tired. "Sit, please," said Sarah. It seemed like ages had passed and the dog wasn't going to understand. Impatiently they waited.

"Sit," said Billy. Just when they were about to give up, she sat and they gave her a food treat. "Good dog," they praised. "Good Fluff." Never give up because your patience pays off.

They also trained her to beg, give paw, sit, stand, fetch, and come. She still did not heal but strained at her leash. They wanted to teach her how to flip, which she did one day unintentionally when she ran after them on her rope to greet them and forgot she was wearing a collar. She did a three sixty flip. Now they would have to find a way to do it without the tether.

When they got tired of their pet, Mom would step in and help. She was a real-life saver when they were in a dull mood of apathy. But usually, they were in bright spirits.

Dad was getting the paper regularly to look for jobs in addition to the computer websites. He left it on the coffee table. Bobby spotted an article, it said, "Circus in Town." He called Billy and Sarah to read it with him.

"Family Circus in town for the month of June. Come one, come all for rides, games, fun, food, and big top entertainment. Big top includes trapeze artists, trained elephants and tigers, clowns, and bicycles through a fire hoop. Find this and much more at Everett's family circus. Admission ten dollars. Open one pm to ten pm daily at the local fair grounds."

They immediately got permission to go. Bobby would watch his younger brother and sister and they would stick together. They would bring Fluff along.

When they got to the circus at one pm it was not really busy with a lot of people yet.

"Let's play a game and see if we can win a prize!" Billy gleefully asked.

So, they went over to the fishbowl area and tried throwing a ping pong ball into a table full of round bowls. A fish was a prize. It was too hard with only one try so they tried several times and it missed. They went to see the animals.

"Oh look, there's the clowns," said Sarah pointing to a circus employee wearing a pink leotard and white tutu.

"That's not a clown, that's an acrobat."

She rushed up to the girl and said "Hi!"

"Hello, how are you doing?"

"I'm fine. Are you a clown?"

"No, but I'm a fellow performer. I do tricks in the air. We have a show at three o'clock. You can see me then."

"I'm sorry to have bothered you," Bobby pled for his sister, "This is her first time at the circus."

"Oh, what a cute dog," Lindalee said. She patted Fluff who let out a loud bark and then growled a little with a snarl. They had never seen her act this way. They apologized and left to walk around. "We'll see you later, sorry she growled, that's unusual for her."

"C'mon," Bobby whispered. "Nice meeting you."

"Likewise."

After walking around awhile and taking in the sights, sounds, and smells, they announced that the big top was ready and people could come watch the performances. They left to go to the big colorful tent.

Bobby, Billy, and Sarah watched mesmerized as a man on a motorbike rode on top of and then in a big circular cage. Plumes of fire leapt out as he rode. Next, there were elephant, bears, and big cat animal performances. It was similar to what they were training Fluff to do. The animals moved through hoops, made pyramid formations with the performers, walked up and down ramps and planks. It was like a magical act with animals. Then they sent in the clowns. They joked around with the music causing everyone to laugh with them and at them at the same time. There was a long pause or hiatus and then the grand finale came. It was the trapeze act. Trapeze artists hung from bars that swung high above the ground. They caught each other by the legs and arms. They had to have perfect timing. There was a safety net that made people breathe easier. "Look, there's Lindalee!" screeched Billy. Sure enough, she was performing up in the air. Everybody clapped, waved, and gasped as she performed. They received an ovation of applause.

After the act was over, the children went to eat a dinner of cotton candy, caramel apples, and funnel cake. As they ate, Bobby made a suggestion, "I wonder if we could get Fluff in on the act and have her perform with the circus."

"Sounds like a bright idea," said Sarah sarcastically.

"No. It's a good idea. Maybe we could get paid for doing it."

So, the children made plans to tell their parents about what they wanted to do and get permission. It was turning to a dusk sky. They hurried home with Fluff. When they got home, they told their Mom and Dad everything that had happened at the circus and what they planned to do to get their dog in on the act. It was agreed that they could inquire about it and try. So, they all slept easier in their beds that night knowing that their dreams of circus fun might come true, and they would have a new story to tell their friends at the end of the summer.

The next day came, and the children had a problem. They didn't have enough money to pay the entrance fees again. "We can't ask Mom and Dad, because it will put them out," said Bobby.

"I know, we can ask Susan or Ronny," Billy suggested.

"No, it's not right because we won't be able to pay them back," replied Sarah. So, they decided to stay home once and for all. They went about their business.

But, when one o'clock rolled around, the start of the circus, a strange thing happened, Fluff grabbed the leash in his mouth and ran with the length of it trailing behind. Bobby started to run after Fluff, then Billy, and then Sarah up the rear, like three ducks chasing a fox. They didn't know where their dog was going but go he must.

They ran and ran afraid their dog was going to be lost. A surprise awaited them at the end. They were at the circus and Fluff dropped the leash where Lindalee stood.

"Good to see you again," said Lindalee, "I see you've lost something," she said petting Fluff whose hairs stood on end.

"Yes, we were going to come here today but we couldn't find the funds for the entrance fee."

"Oh, I can arrange that." Lindalee spoke with the ticket booth operator, and he let them in for free due to official business.

"There's something more we'd like to ask of you," said Bobby. "We'd like to have Fluff audition for the circus."

"That can be arranged, we have a break coming up in twenty minutes. I'll get my Dad, who is the ringmaster and he'll watch you kids and your dog do his stuff."

"Agreed." They waited and practiced with Fluff. Luckily Sarah had a bag of treats in her pocket that they could use.

Twenty minutes passed quickly, they went into the ring.

"Meet Rally, my Dad the ringmaster," said Lindalee.

"Okay kids, do your stuff."

"For our first trick, Fluff will sit."

"Sit. Fluff," said Sarah. She had done it many times before, but Fluff wouldn't sit. "Okay, stand Fluff." Thank you Fluff, she gave the dog a treat. Billy stifled a giggle at the joke. "Paw Fluff," said Sarah nervously. After a moment's hesitation Fluff gave paw. The children were relieved. "Beg Fluff," the dog begged. They threw a small hoop, "Fetch Fluff." Fluff retrieved the ring! Sarah walked away, "Come here Fluff." The dog responded. "That's it," said Bobby. "We are working on a flip trick where the dog does a turn in the air."

Rally consulted his daughter. "We do need a tie-in act after the animals and before the clowns. You can dress Fluff as a clown and do your stuff to a little music. It doesn't pay much, but if you are successful, you get a raise."

"Thank you, thank you so much," the children effused joyfully.

"Stick around, you start tonight."

The children phoned their parents and told them about their success. Then they went to get costumes. Lindalee took the children and their dog to get suited up in their costumes. Fluff went first. She had a blue, mini, conical hat with a pink pom pom on top and a fluffy pink rim. She had a matching doggy jacket that shimmered like satin.

The children had a similar color and theme. All of a sudden, a fear struck Sarah. She thought of all the people's eyes on her and she had what is called stage fright. Lindalee tried to soothe, "The lights will be on you and you won't see anybody, try to pretend that you are alone just doing your regular tasks."

"I'm still scared," said Sarah.

"Okay, I'll dress up and be on standby."

It was just as Lindalee said. She dressed up and went in with them to perform their act.

"And now we have… Clown Fluff and her entourage." People clapped and the children went to the center of the ring and waved to the audience.

"Sit… beg… paw… fetch… come…" The audience clapped and laughed.

"Thank you, thank you… Let's give a big round of applause for Fluff and her friends. That was a first-time performance for them," Rally announced.

The children got out of costume. They thanked Lindalee who gave them fifty dollars. They said their goodbyes and promised to be back tomorrow. They were eager to tell Mom and Dad how they did.

"Mom, Dad, we performed!" they chimed.

"Great," said Mom, "Did you get paid?"

"Yes, fifty dollars!"

"Wow, that's great."

"Kids, I don't want you to go back to the circus," Dad said.

"Why not?" they asked.

"Because I want to be the one to provide for you. I'm supposed to be the breadwinner. How does this look, making my kids into a circus act."

"We are not doing it for money, we are doing it for fun."

"Dad, the kids are right. They are learning work skills and need an outlet for all their energy. I support them."

"Okay then," Dad conceded.

Mom gave them a big cardboard box that she had decorated and showed them a new trick with Fluff. She put the opening toward Fluff and said, "Get in the box." She waved her arm toward the box. Fluff listened. When the children tried it, it didn't work quite as well, but they would use it in their act. If worse came to worse, they could throw a dog treat or stick into the box so she would obey.

They tried to teach Fluff how to flip by saying Flip and having her sit, beg, and then lifting her up and guiding her through the overturn. It seemed impossible without her running with the rope. But with the rope it seemed abusive. The children tired.

"This doesn't look like it's going to work," griped Sarah. She dejectedly threw her used bubblegum into the back yard grass. Fluff rooted for it and started to chew. "No, Fluff, spit it out." But before she could remove it a bubble was blown by Fluff. They all laughed, Mom and Dad included.

They looked into using the leash as a flipping agent with the veterinarian. She said it was risky but with a padded collar was probably harmless since she did it before without any injury.

The children went back to the circus with three new tricks: the box trick, flip, and bubble gum. They were happy. But when they got to the circus that day, Lindalee was in tears, and I mean real tears not clown tears.

"What's the matter Lindalee," they questioned.

"Oh, nothing."

"Yes, it must be something."

"Okay, I'll own up. Last year my timing on the trapeze was a few seconds off and my partner fell and sprained his leg. They wanted me to quit and start my own clown act. But I didn't want to dress like no ugly, silly clown. Sob, sob. So, they bought me a dog and I threw it into the dump. I lied and said it had run away by accident."

The children were stunned. Fluff barked twice as in confirmation of the story.

"Now that you are all here, I see it's not that bad to be a clown after all. People love clowns and you are doing your part to make them feel good. Can I join your act?"

"Sure, you can," mystery solved.

They were all pretty sure that Fluff was the original circus act dog. They confirmed this fact with Rally and Lindalee. But to their surprise the story wasn't over yet. It turned out that there was a ten-thousand-dollar reward for the safe return of the animal, which the children won. But, they wanted to keep the dog as their own. So, an arrangement was worked out and they could keep the dog but would allow her to perform with the circus.

Mom and Dad used the money to pay some bills and put the rest of the money into the children's college fund. They put on a block party to celebrate. Ronny, Susan, Rally, and Lindalee came along with some of their schoolmates. It was the best summer ever.

Back at the circus, they had perfected their dog clown act. It went something like this: "Ladies and Gentlemen, let me introduce you to Flippin' Fluff." The children took their places. The audience cheered. "Fluff sit," she sat. "Fluff paw," she shook paw. "May I have a volunteer from the audience?" they picked a young child who led the dog through fetching by throwing a baton. "Get in the box." Fluff went in the wildly decorated box. "Out, out." Finally, when they tapped the box to everyone's amazement and laughter she walked out of the box. She blew her bubble gum bubble. Then they put her in a red bucket by the trapeze ladder. Lindalee had already climbed the ladder and hoisted the bucket with a rope and a pulley. When Fluff reached the top, everyone cheered.

"We are now going to flip Fluff." Lindalee and her partner trapeze artist were going to throw Fluff into a flip and then catch her on the other side. She would be the first dog ever as a part of a trapeze act. "Drum roll please." "Here we go." Lindalee swung from the trapeze bar, at precisely the right moment she let go of the dog and Fluff twirled in the air, then her partner grabbed Fluff by the forelegs after she came out of the spin. They dog was placed on the top podium. "Let's hear it for Flippin' Fluff." There was a standing ovation.

One day near the end of the summer, the children couldn't find Fluff. She wasn't in her doghouse. They searched around their house and yard, but no Fluff. Finally, they decided to go to the circus. When they got to the circus, they still couldn't find her.

"Did anyone check the box?" Billy asked. He ran over to the box and looked inside. It was Fluff with eight puppies!

"Quick go get Lindalee." Lindalee brought a small rug and blanket to keep the pups warm. They were so tiny and funny looking because they were newborns.

"Fluff is a Mom," said Sarah. She posted the dogs pictures on her computer website page. They were all healthy and lived to adulthood. They gave one pup to Susan, on pup to Ronny, one pup to the mailman, and Mr. Rasseter. Circus people adopted and found homes for the others. They would in the future become part of the act too.

They spent the rest of the year doing their work and cuddling in their beds with Fluff and her puppies the rest of the time. They had a lot in common with the kids at school now, and that helped them make new friends. Dad finally got a dream job after he went to school to learn about computers. Mom ran a fan club for Fluff, because after people found out about her story they wanted to keep in touch and have a picture of Fluff.

They were well off now and would never have to search in the dumpster for food again. Plus, they had made true friends of Susan, Ronny, the postman, Lindalee, and Rally. That my friends is the whole story, total Fluff!

THE END. . .